the Salamander Room

by ANNE MAZER
illustrated by STEVE JOHNSON & LOU FANCHER

Dragonfly Books 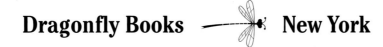 New York

All rights reserved. Published in the United States by Dragonfly Books, an imprint of
Random House Children's Books, a division of Random House, Inc., New York.
Originally published in hardcover in the United States by Alfred A. Knopf, an imprint of
Random House Children's Books, a division of Random House, Inc., New York, in 1991.

Dragonfly Books with the colophon is a registered trademark of Random House, Inc.

Visit us on the Web! www.randomhouse.com/kids

Educators and librarians, for a variety of teaching tools, visit us at www.randomhouse.com/teachers

The Library of Congress has cataloged the hardcover edition of this work as follows:
Mazer, Anne.
The salamander room / by Anne Mazer ; illustrated by Steve Johnson.
Summary: A young boy finds a salamander and thinks of the many things
he can do to make a perfect home for it.
ISBN 978-0-394-82945-6 (trade) — ISBN 978-0-394-92945-3 (lib. bdg.)
[1. Salamanders—Fiction. 2. Ecology—Fiction.]
I. Johnson, Steve, ill.
PZ7.M47396 Sal 1991
[E]—20
90033301

ISBN 978-0-679-86187-4 (pbk.)

Book design by Lou Fancher

MANUFACTURED IN CHINA

36 35

For Mollie

A. M.

For Joel, Erin, Dale, and Tessa,
and a special thanks to Dave R.

S. J. & L. F.

Brian found a salamander in the woods. It was a little orange salamander that crawled through the dried leaves of the forest floor.

The salamander was warm and cozy in the boy's hand. "Come live with me," Brian said.

He took the salamander home.

"Where will he sleep?" his mother asked.

"I will make him a salamander bed to sleep in. I will cover him with leaves that are fresh and green, and bring moss that looks like little stars to be a pillow for his head. I will bring crickets to sing him to sleep and bullfrogs to tell him good-night stories."

"And when he wakes up, where will he play?"

"I will carpet my room with shiny wet leaves
and water them so he can slide around and play.

I will bring tree stumps into
my room so he can climb up the bark
and sun himself on top. And I will bring
boulders that he can creep over."

"He will miss his friends in the forest."

"I will bring salamander friends to play with him."

"They will be hungry. How will you feed them?"

"I will bring insects to live in my room. And every day I will catch some and feed the salamanders. And I will make little pools of water on top of the boulders so they can drink whenever they are thirsty."

"The insects will multiply, and soon there will be bugs and insects everywhere."

"I will find birds to eat the extra bugs and insects. And the bullfrogs will eat them too."

"Where will the birds and bullfrogs live?"

"I will bring trees for the birds to roost in,
and make ponds for the frogs."

"Birds need to fly."

"We can lift off the ceiling. They will sail out in the sky, but they will come back to my room when it is time for dinner, because they will know that the biggest, juiciest insects are there."

"But the trees—how will they grow?"

"The rain will come through the open roof,
and the sun, too. And vines will
creep up the walls of my room,
and ferns will grow under my bed.
There will be big white mushrooms
and moss like little stars growing around
the tree stumps that the salamanders climb on."

"And you—
where will you sleep?"

"I will sleep on a bed under
the stars, with the moon
shining through the green
leaves of the trees; owls will
hoot and crickets will sing;
and next to me, on the
boulder with its head resting
on soft moss, the salamander
will sleep."